THE THERMECINE ROAD

JT BALDWIN

"The most effective weapons are those who believe they chose their target. A properly developed asset will pursue objectives with genuine conviction, never recognizing the careful architecture of their motivation. Love, properly applied, becomes the most reliable form of control."

— From "Network Development: Advanced Techniques" (Stonewake Group Internal Document

Series Guide | THE PALISADE JOURNALS

RECOMMENDED READING ORDER:

CHRONOLOGICAL TIMELINE:

- 2173 | *I, Marked*
  A girl named Anne becomes a weapon called Snips.

- ▶ **2178 | *The Thermecine Road* ◀ You Are Here**
  Regal Eldain begins his descent down the road of vengeance.

- 2183 | *Test of Character*
  Victoria Colwell witnesses an unspeakable transfer of power.

- 2189 | *Fortune Forged*
  Peri Blackwood's first con and the cost of leadership.

- 2191 | *Chief Minister*
  The highest office is not enough for Shori Ashford.

PART ONE

Broken Steel

Late Winter, 2178

Northern Territories, Continental Authority Border

— ❖ —

The sky bled gray over the ruins of the old rail yard.

Regal Eldain stumbled through the wreckage, boots crunching over brittle ice and rusted rails half-buried in frozen mud. Each breath burned. Vapor curled from cracked lips into air cold enough to make his teeth ache. Snowmelt dripped from the skeletons of shattered cargo cars in slow, steady beats. The sound of a clock winding down.

The cold had stopped mattering hours ago. His fingers were numb, clumsy against the wound in his side. Fresh blood seeped through the makeshift bandage, warmer than the air, steaming faintly where it met the chill. Three days on the run. The bleeding hadn't stopped.

She sagged against him. Barely conscious.

He adjusted his grip around her shoulders. Dragged her weight higher. Forced one more step. Then another. Her skin burned with fever against his arm, the heat of her wrong against the frozen world around them. Two years locked in their cells had done this. Muscles gone. Weight gone. Sixteen years old and she looked twelve, hollowed out from the inside by people who'd kept her alive only because what ran through her veins was worth keeping.

"We're almost there," Regal murmured.

Neither of them believed it.

A gutted maintenance shack ahead. Roof half-collapsed, one wall leaning at a bad angle. The corrugated metal siding was streaked with decades of rust and the kind of neglect that said nobody had needed this place in a long time. Shelter enough. Barely.

He shoved the door open with his shoulder. The hinges shrieked. Nobody came running. Just the wind threading through holes in the walls, finding every gap in the structure the way cold always found gaps.

He lowered her to the floor against the most intact wall. Careful. Slower than the cold wanted him to be. She curled in on herself and a sound came out of her, low and broken, the kind of sound that doesn't have words because words would require energy she'd stopped having days ago.

Regal stripped off his coat and wrapped it around her. Tucked the edges close. Made sure the collar covered her neck where the cold would find the blood vessels closest to the surface. His hands were clumsy with numbness but they were careful. More careful than they'd been with anything else in weeks. More careful than they'd be with anything else again.

A curl of blonde hair slipped free across her forehead. Darker than he remembered. The golden color dulled to something closer to straw, two years without sunlight leaching the brightness out of it the way it had leached everything else. He brushed it back. His gloved hand too big, too rough for the gesture. But gentle. The particular gentleness of someone who understood that the thing they were touching was the only thing left in the world they couldn't afford to break.

Her eyes fluttered open. Just for a moment.

Rust. Not brown, not hazel. Rust. The color of old iron left in weather, but alive somehow, with a metallic quality underneath that caught what little light reached them through the broken roof. A faint reflection, like looking at something through tarnished copper. The color that had marked her. The color that had brought the hunters to their door.

Her eyes closed. The effort of opening them was more than she could maintain.

Still breathing. Still fighting.

Good.

Regal turned to the pile of moldering crates stacked against the far wall. His movements were mechanical. Habit driving a body that had stopped consulting with the mind operating it. He broke the driest planks apart, splintering them into kindling with hands that left blood on the wood. The lighter was in his jacket pocket where it always was. Brass. Refillable. The flint wheel was stiff from the cold and it took three tries before the flame caught.

He fed it carefully. Splinters first. Then the larger pieces. The patience of a man who understood that fire was the difference between alive and not, and that the difference was thinner than the flame.

The fire burned in a rusted metal barrel. Flames casting shadows across the broken walls. Smoke seeped through the gaps in the roof. Risky. But without heat, the conversation about risk was academic.

He gathered her and moved her closer to the warmth. Positioned himself between her and the direct heat, shielding her the way you shield a wound. Let the warmth reach her gradually. Not too fast. A body this cold, warmed too quickly, could stop.

Only then did he allow himself to sit.

He sank against the opposite wall. The breath that came out of him was closer to a groan than he wanted it to be. His side throbbed. Deep. Relentless. He peeled back the sodden cloth and looked at what was underneath. The wound was ragged, deep enough that the edges didn't want to stay together, still weeping in the slow persistent way that meant something inside hadn't sealed. He bound it tighter with what he had left. Stopgap on top of a stopgap.

That was when he saw it.

The axe.

What was left of it. The shattered remains of his father's axe lay on the floor beside him where it had fallen from his pack. The blue-tinted steel, dulled and splintered, the head cracked nearly in half. The haft broken clean through. His father had forged that steel in a shop that smelled like coal smoke and hot metal and the particular patience of a man who understood that good work took the time it took. Blue-tinted because of the process. Something in the way his father treated the metal during the final quench, a technique he'd learned from his father, who'd learned it from his. The axe had split wood and cleared brush and hung above the fireplace and eventually, when the world demanded it, done worse.

Now it was scrap. The head in two pieces. The haft in three.

Something inside Regal cracked with it.

The roar tore out of his chest before he could stop it. He grabbed the broken axe and hurled it across the shack. It slammed into the far wall with a hollow clatter. Shards of wood scattered across the concrete floor.

She stirred at the noise. Didn't wake. Her breathing rattled. Thin but steady.

Regal pressed his forehead against the cold siding. His fists clenched until the torn knuckles bled fresh.

And memory dragged him under.

✿

The alarm bell clanged overhead. Mechanical rhythm pounding against white walls. Regal pressed his back against cold concrete, the axe gripped tight in bleeding hands. Bodies behind him. Union guards who'd stood in the wrong corridor.

Another intersection. Another guess. The facility was a labyrinth, concrete and fluorescent lighting and corridors that looked identical, designed to disorient, to trap, to make a man with an axe feel like a rat in a box.

A scream cut through the noise. High and thin.

He ran toward it.

The laboratory door hung half-open. Inside: white coats around a table. Strapped to it, a figure. Thin. Wild-haired. Pale against the sterile white. Tubes threaded from her arms to machines that hummed with a purpose he didn't understand, drawing something from her blood into glass vials that caught the fluorescent light with a faint metallic sheen.

They looked up too late.

The axe bit deep.

What followed was blood and steel and shouting and then silence.

He didn't bother with the restraints' mechanisms. The axe solved that too.

"Can you walk?" he asked.

Weak fingers clutched at his sleeve.

Heavy boots thundering in the corridor outside.

Regal lifted her. Light as kindling. Broken weight against his chest.

"Hold on. Whatever happens, we're leaving."

✿

The memory faded. Pain, cold, and the hiss of snow against broken windows.

The Enforcer's blade. The clash. The shattering of the axe head against steel that should not have held.

The wound tearing into his side.

The desperate flight through wastelands where even the dead offered no shelter.

And before all of it. The fire. The screams. The family he couldn't save.

Because of her.

Because of Shori Ashford.

He spat the name into the dirt. Bitter as the blood in his mouth.

She would pay.

All of them would pay.

When the shaking in his hands faded, Regal forced himself upright. His legs trembled. They held.

He crossed the shack and knelt by what was left of the axe. The pieces lay where they'd hit. Blue-tinted steel catching the firelight through the grime, the color still there despite the damage, the particular shade his father's technique had given it.

Gently. Almost reverently. He wrapped the pieces in a strip of cloth. The largest shard of steel still held its edge on one side. Even broken, the quality of the work was visible. Even shattered, it was his father's hands in the metal.

He tucked the bundle into his pack and cinched it tight against his back.

Then he turned to her.

She was still curled under his coat. The firelight moved across her face, the shadows filling the hollows that captivity had carved beneath her cheekbones. Her breathing had steadied. The rattle was still there but quieter. The warmth was doing something.

He knelt beside her. Adjusted the coat. His hands moving with the same care he'd used on the axe, the same reverence, as if both things were sacred and both things were broken and both things were the only pieces of his old life that had survived.

"We need to move," he said. Softer than his voice went for anyone else. Softer than it would go again.

She stirred. Her eyes opened for a moment. Rust, catching the firelight, the metallic quality underneath giving the color a depth that shifted with the flame.

"No," she whispered. Curling deeper into the coat. "Please. Too tired."

"I know." He tucked a strand of hair behind her ear. The gesture too tender for his hands, too tender for this place, too tender for the man he was becoming. "But they're coming. We can't stay."

She shook her head. Her fingers clutched at the coat. The effort of gripping the fabric was visible in her face. Two years had stolen everything from her except the ability to hold on to what was closest.

Regal sighed. No anger in it. Just the sound of a man accepting weight.

"We don't have far to go," he lied. His voice was kind. It wouldn't always be. "I'll get you somewhere safe."

Her eyes found his. Rust meeting dark brown. A flicker of trust in someone who had every reason to trust nothing.

"Rest against me. I'll carry you."

He wrapped his coat tighter around her. Lifted her. She settled against his chest, her head tucking beneath his chin. The gesture of a child seeking shelter, and of someone who had learned that the only safe place in the world was the space between his arms.

He kicked snow over the fire. It died with a final hiss. The shack went dark.

One step into the cold. Then another.

The frozen waste opened around them. White and gray and empty. The wind pushing against his chest like something trying to stop him. His side bleeding. His hands numb. His legs carrying weight they shouldn't have been able to carry because the alternative was setting her down and he was not going to set her down.

Regal Eldain walked into the dark. Behind him, the ruins of the rail yard. Ahead, nothing he could see.

The fury was there. It was always there. Aimed at every piece of a world that had taken everything from him.

But not at her. Never at the weight in his arms.

She was the only thing he could still carry without breaking.

PART TWO

ROADS OF ICE

Late Winter, 2178

Halstrom Entry, Continental Authority Border

Five days. That's how long it had taken for Regal's hands to stop shaking.

Not from the cold. That passed.

Not from the blood loss. That would come again.

From what he couldn't fix. The memory of her burning with fever, light as kindling in his arms. The sound of her breathing getting thinner with each step through the frozen dark. The moment he'd finally reached the farmstead and Marta had taken her from him, and his arms had gone empty, and the weight he'd been carrying was gone, and somehow that was worse.

He hadn't seen her since. Five days in the back room of Marta and Joren's cabin, sleeping and bleeding and sleeping again, while she recovered somewhere else in the house. He could hear her sometimes through the walls. Coughing. Moving. Once, in the middle of the night, a sound that might have been crying or might have been something else.

He didn't go to her. Didn't know what he'd say if he did. Didn't know if the person he'd find would still be the person he'd carried.

Dawn spilled through the warped cabin windows, pale and brittle. He gathered what little remained: fresh bandages. A clean shirt. The broken axe, wrapped in oilcloth. And the metal case he'd taken from the Ossuary. He hadn't opened it yet.

Behind him, Marta clattered dishes with too much force. The sound carried blame she was too kind to put into words. Her husband, Joren, stood in the doorway, arms folded, saying nothing the way men say nothing when they've already decided what they think.

"That poor child. We're so sorry."

Something in her tone made Regal stop packing. "She'll recover."

Marta and Joren exchanged a look.

"What?" Regal demanded.

Joren's jaw worked. He was choosing words the way a man chooses where to step in bad terrain. "The fever broke three days ago. But the girl's eyes..." He trailed off. Started again. "They're different."

"Different how?"

"The color's changed. Gotten more intense." Joren rubbed the back of his neck. "That rust color, it was always unusual. But now there's something behind it. A shine. Metallic, almost. Like copper left on a hot stove. It catches the lamplight wrong."

"That's not new," Regal said, but the words came out with less certainty than he wanted.

"It is," Marta said quietly. "Before, the color was just color. Now it looks like something's behind it. And her hands..." She held up her own, turning them over. "They're warm. Too warm. Like running a fever, except she's not feverish anymore. The temperature is just there. Constant."

Regal's hand found the knife at his belt. Reflex. "What are you saying?"

"She stares at nothing for hours," Joren said. "Sits by the window and watches the tree line like she's waiting for something we can't see. Doesn't blink. Doesn't move. Mycha sits with her, talks to her, and she responds normally enough. But then she goes back to the window."

The silence in the kitchen was heavy.

"Who's watching her now?" Regal asked.

"Mycha. She knows what to do." Marta's voice softened. "We'll keep her safe and comfortable. But whatever they did to her at the Ossuary..." She shook her head. "It's not finished. It's still doing something to her."

"You have our word she'll be protected," Joren said. "But you need to find answers. Soon. Before whatever's happening gets past where answers can help."

Regal looked at them. Friends of his father. Good people. Strong enough to have helped him prepare for the raid, old enough that the cost of helping showed in their faces. He saw fear in their eyes. Not of him. For her.

He couldn't stay. Not when staying meant watching whatever was happening unfold and not being able to stop it.

He nodded. Shouldered his pack. Walked into the bitter morning.

He didn't look back. If he looked back, he'd go to her, and if he went to her, he'd stay, and if he stayed, he'd be useless. Better to be moving. Better to be doing something, even if the something was walking south with no plan and no allies and a wound in his side that hadn't sealed.

※

The tavern was the kind of place that existed in border towns like a stain that couldn't be scrubbed out. Dim. Smoky. Populated by people who had either given up or hadn't started yet. Regal fit both descriptions.

A fourth drink. A fifth. The Ossuary. Joren's words about her eyes. The weight of everything he'd done and everything that still needed doing. It circled. The alcohol didn't quiet it. Just numbed the edges enough that the pain in his side dropped from a scream to a grind.

"You're not from around here."

Heavyset man. Union garrison tattoo on his forearm, faded and weathered but unmistakable. Discharged, probably. Still carrying the posture.

Regal stared into his glass. "Just passing through."

"Funny time of year to be traveling." The man leaned closer. Alcohol on his breath. "Unless you're running from something."

Two more drifted over. Smelling entertainment the way dogs smell blood. Former soldiers by the way they held their shoulders.

"I'm not looking for trouble," Regal said. The lie sat bitter on his tongue. Trouble was exactly what he wanted. Something simple. Something that hit back. Something that existed in his body instead of his head.

The first one grinned. "Bit late for that. You've got that Freehold look about you."

Regal could have walked away. Should have.

He finished his drink. Set the glass down.

"And you've got that Union stink."

He threw the first punch before the glass stopped rocking. A jab to the leader's throat that sent him reeling into the bar. Regal grabbed a chair and swung it into the second man's ribs. Wood cracked. The man folded.

Two down. One behind him.

The third man caught him around the neck. Arm locked. Regal's feet left the ground for a second before he drove an elbow back and connected with something that crunched. The grip loosened. He twisted free.

But the leader had recovered. His fist found Regal's side. The wound. The one that was five days into healing and not close to healed.

White. Everything went white. Then the floor was coming up and Regal's hands were too slow to catch himself and his head hit the edge of the bar on the way down.

After that it was boots and fists and the shouting of the tavern keeper and his father's training kicking in between the gaps where his body still listened. A block that worked. A strike that didn't. The taste of blood and the particular sound of someone hitting you when you're already down and they're enjoying it.

Cold air. Dragged outside. A final kick that sent him down an embankment into a ditch. Half-frozen runoff and mud. The cold hitting him like a second beating.

"Welcome to Union territory, Freehold trash."

Laughter. Boots on gravel. Fading.

Regal lay face-down in the icy water and didn't move.

Pain came in waves. The side wound bleeding fresh, turning the water pink around him. Cold seeping through his clothes and into the parts of him that the fight hadn't already numbed. One eye swelling shut. Ribs grinding in a way that meant something was cracked or broken or both.

He stayed there. Minutes. Maybe longer. The twilight deepening around him. Water in his boots. His fingers going numb. The image of rust-colored eyes staring at a tree line, waiting for something nobody else could see, while he lay in a ditch bleeding because he'd picked a fight with three men for no reason except that he needed something to hit.

When he finally moved, it was because something was digging into his ribs from inside his jacket. The metal case.

His fingers were half-frozen and clumsy. He nearly dropped it into the muddy water. The case was small, smooth, the surface unmarred despite everything it had been through. He'd taken it from the Ossuary during the escape. Grabbed it off a table in the laboratory where they'd been drawing from her blood. Hadn't thought about why. Just took it.

He turned it over, looking for a way in. In his frustration, he cracked it against a stone jutting from the ditch bank.

A thin seam appeared along one edge. Another blow widened it. He wedged his thumbnail in.

The case split open.

Inside: a glass vial. Three ounces, maybe. A brownish-green liquid, murky, with particles suspended in it that moved when the vial moved. Not like water. Thicker. The particles drifting in slow patterns that followed the motion of his hand with a slight delay, the way sediment follows current.

The same substance he'd seen in the laboratory machines. The stuff they'd been pulling from her blood.

He held the vial up against the fading sky. No markings. No labels. Just the murky fluid and the particles inside it.

He watched it for a long time. Tried to understand what he was looking at. The particles moved differently when his hands were steady versus when they shook. Settled when he held still. Stirred when he shifted. Could be vibration. Could be the warmth of his grip changing the viscosity. Could be something else he didn't have the vocabulary to name.

Whatever it was, it had been inside her. And now it was in a vial in his hand in a ditch on the side of a road.

He wrapped it carefully and put it in his jacket pocket. Close to his body. Where it would stay warm.

◎

The boarding house was cheap, anonymous, and warm. The proprietor took his money and didn't ask about his face. Smart man. Or tired man. Same thing in a border town.

The room was small. One bed, one table, one chair, a bathroom with water that took three minutes to turn from brown to clear. Regal peeled off his clothes and stood under the shower until the heat ran out, watching the water turn pink and then clear around his feet.

His body in the mirror afterward: a map of recent damage layered over older scars. The Ossuary wound in his side, reopened, angry. A fresh gash on his thigh from the ditch. Bruises darkening across his ribs in the shape of boot treads. His face swollen on the left side, the eye nearly closed. Twenty years old and he looked like something that had been used hard and put away wet.

He cleaned and bandaged what he could reach. Did a bad job of it because his hands were still clumsy and the angle on the side wound was wrong and he didn't have anyone to hold the gauze while he wrapped.

He'd had someone once. His father's hands, steady and practiced, bandaging a cut from the forge when Regal was twelve. "Hold still. It won't scar if you hold still." It scarred anyway. Everything scarred.

When the wounds were dressed, he set the vial on the table.

The liquid inside had settled during the walk to the boarding house. The particles drifting in slow, regular patterns. He leaned close. Watched. The movement was consistent. Rhythmic, almost. Responding to something, though whether it was the vibration of his breathing or the heat of his proximity or something else entirely, he couldn't tell.

The substance had come from her blood. Whatever the Ossuary had been doing to her, this was part of it. And according to Marta, whatever they'd started was still working. Still changing her.

He wrapped the vial in a clean cloth and put it in his pack.

Morning found him with a map spread on the table, the weak light barely enough to read by. Braelocke Hollow. Five days south on foot. A settlement on the border between Union and Independent territories, reached by rough roads through terrain that discouraged casual travel. Joren had mentioned it once, years ago. "If you ever need medicine that doesn't exist in any official catalog, that's where you'd look. Or the people who know how to make it."

If anyone could tell him what this substance was and what it was doing to her, they'd be there.

Regal packed. Every movement cost him. The ribs. The side. The thigh. His body filing complaints he couldn't address because the alternative was sitting still, and sitting still meant thinking, and thinking meant the ditch and the tavern and the rust-colored eyes staring at nothing.

He stepped onto the road. Sun clearing the horizon. Long shadows on frozen ground.

Five days to Braelocke Hollow.

One step. Then another.

PART THREE

THE HOLLOW'S BARGAIN

Early Spring, 2178

Braelocke Hollow, Border Territories

The settlement guards at the gate eyed Regal with the particular disdain reserved for obvious trouble. Five days of walking had done what five days of walking does to a man with a wound gone septic: stripped the weight off him, put a flush on his cheeks, and taught him a new way to hold his left side that fooled nobody.

"Entry fee's three bronze tokens," the guard said. "Medical clearance is extra if you're carrying anything contagious."

"I'm not sick," Regal lied. He produced his last coins.

"Sure you're not." The guard pocketed them. "Try not to bleed on anything valuable."

Braelocke Hollow sprawled ahead of him. A patchwork of concrete and corrugated metal, built in the gaps between Union control and Freehold authority. The Fractured Bazaar occupied the center: stalls crammed into every available space between repurposed shipping containers, vendors hawking salvaged machinery and questionable medicines under awnings made from whatever kept the rain off.

Regal wandered the market. Asked questions. Got the responses he deserved.

"Pre-collapse materials?" A weapons dealer laughed at him. "You writing a report for someone, boy?"

"I'm just curious about..."

"Curiosity like that gets people disappeared. Move along."

His approach was as subtle as his depot raid would be. Direct questions to strangers, no cover story, no reason for anyone to trust him and plenty of reasons not to. Three vendors shut him down. Two quoted prices he couldn't pay. One just looked at him like he was already dead and hadn't figured it out yet.

"You've got that look," someone said behind him.

Thin man. Scarred face. One good eye that moved faster than the rest of him. Gaunt in the way that said either illness or discipline, and the way he carried himself said discipline. Someone used to being small and using it.

"What look?" Regal asked.

"The look of a man who found something he doesn't understand." The stranger settled at a nearby table without asking. "Name's Davyl. And you've been asking half the bazaar about unusual materials and pre-collapse identification services." He grinned. Gap-toothed. "Subtle as a brick through a window, you are."

Regal's hand went to his jacket pocket. Reflex.

"Course you don't know what I'm talking about." Davyl's grin widened. "That's why three vendors have already marked you as Union bait or easy prey. Lucky for you, I'm in a generous mood."

Desperation sat Regal down at the table before his instincts could stop him.

"What do you want?"

"To help. For a price." Davyl waved at a serving girl. "See, information's currency in Braelocke. But good information only flows to people who've earned it. You want answers? You need to prove you're worth the risk."

The proposition was simple. The Union supply depot on Braelocke's eastern edge. Telegraph detonators in storage. Steal them. Bring them back. Proof of competence. Then Davyl could connect him with people who might know about the substance in the vial.

Simple grab, Davyl said. Minimal risk.

Regal, feverish and out of options, heard only the promise of answers.

✧

The Union supply depot squatted on Braelocke's eastern edge. Concrete walls. Razor wire. Guard posts at two corners, manned by soldiers who looked bored enough to be dangerous.

Regal spent fifteen minutes studying it. A professional would have mapped guard rotations, identified security weaknesses, planned entry and exit routes, timed the patrols, found the gap. Regal decided fifteen minutes was enough.

He went in through the front.

The gate guard died before the alarm. Regal's knife found the gap between his collar and his jaw, a move that was more desperation than technique. The guard made a sound like a clogged drain and went down. The second guard had time to shout. Not time to do anything about it.

After that: alarms. The shriek of mechanical bells overhead, the kind that couldn't be silenced from a panel because there was no panel. Boots on concrete. Shouting. The corridors were industrial, fluorescent lights and painted block walls, everything designed for function and nothing designed for a man with a knife trying to navigate by dead reckoning and Davyl's hand-drawn map.

He found the storage room. Telegraph detonators in wooden crates, packed in straw, smaller than he'd expected. He grabbed two. Shoved them in his jacket.

The first soldier came around the corner as Regal was leaving the room. The knife solved that. The second soldier came from the other direction. The knife solved that too, but it cost Regal a cut across his forearm that immediately started bleeding in the fast, bright way that meant something important had been nicked.

The exit was not the entrance. The exit was a window. Regal went through it shoulder-first, taking the glass with him, landing in mud and broken concrete on the other side.

He ran. Behind him, more alarms. More boots. More shouting. A round cracked off the wall above his head. Ammunition spent on him. He didn't have time to appreciate the compliment.

He should have been caught. Should have been killed. Only Union incompetence and sheer dumb luck got him to the rendezvous point alive.

He arrived bleeding from the forearm, the glass cuts, the reopened side wound, and two new injuries he hadn't noticed yet. The detonators in his jacket were intact. The rest of him was not.

✧

The meeting place wasn't the tavern Davyl had suggested. A hastily scrawled note redirected him to a warehouse in the industrial district. Concrete walls. Loading dock. The kind of building that existed for purposes its owners didn't discuss.

The door opened to reveal not Davyl, but a woman.

Regal's first thought was not about how she looked. It was about the temperature. The warehouse was cold, the same industrial cold that lived in every concrete building in Braelocke. But where she stood, the air felt different. Closer. Warmer. As if her presence had mass and the space around her had adjusted to accommodate it.

She was not tall. Dark auburn hair pulled back. Green eyes that found him in the doorway and didn't move off him. Clothes that were practical but better than anything in Braelocke: clean seams, good fabric, the kind of quality that said resources without advertising them.

"You must be Davyl's latest project." She stepped aside to let him enter. Her voice was educated. Inner territories accent. "I was expecting someone more intact."

"I got what he asked for." Regal produced the detonators. His hands were clumsy. The blood loss and the fever and the proximity of a person who was warm and close and looking at him with attention he hadn't experienced from anyone who wasn't trying to kill him.

"Yes, but at what cost?" She gestured at the blood soaking through his shirt. "Half the garrison is looking for whoever butchered their supply depot. That's not theft. That's advertisement."

The warehouse interior was functional. Chairs. A table. Supplies against one wall. She moved to pour herself a drink from a bottle that would have cost more than Regal's entry fee.

"Drink?" She glanced back at him.

"Who are you?" Regal asked.

"Someone who might be able to help you." She sat. "Or might decide you're too dangerous to leave breathing. Depends on what you tell me next."

She watched him the way he'd watched the depot: assessing points of entry, structural weaknesses, what it would cost to get inside. The difference was that she was better at it than him, and she wasn't trying to hide the assessment.

"Davyl said..."

"Davyl says whatever serves his purposes. I'm more interested in yours." Her green eyes held his. "What were you really doing at that depot?"

Regal hesitated. Then he pulled the vial from his inner pocket. The murky liquid shifted when it moved, the particles inside following the motion with their slow, delayed drift.

"I need to know what this is."

Something changed in her face. Not her expression. Behind her expression. A sharpening that had nothing to do with the vial's appearance and everything to do with what it meant. She recognized it, or recognized something about it. That reaction lasted less than a second before she controlled it.

"Where did you find it?"

"The Ossuary."

"If you're going to lie to me..."

"I can prove it."

She questioned him for twenty minutes. Methods. Goals. Background. Every answer exposed how little he knew and how much he'd risked without knowing it. She didn't bother hiding her assessment of his amateur status.

"You freed someone from there," she said. "Someone important to you."

"That's not your concern."

"It is if I'm going to help you. The Ossuary isn't just a prison. It's a processing facility. They don't keep people there. They change them." Her eyes moved across his face, reading something in the set of his jaw, the position of his hands. "The fact that you got anyone out alive suggests either luck or more capability than you're showing me right now."

"You seem well-informed about their operations," Regal said.

A pause. Brief enough to miss if he hadn't been watching. "Information networks. You learn things when you make a living staying ahead of institutional power."

Before she could continue, the warehouse door slammed open.

Three men. The lead was tall and heavyset, carrying scars like credentials. The other two fanned to his sides with the practiced spacing of people who'd done this enough to skip the rehearsal.

"Well, well." The leader took in the scene. "Lathim sends his regards."

"Davyl's boss?" Regal asked. His hand moved to his knife.

"Davyl's banker. And you've got a price on your head, friend. Union's offering good coin for whoever tore up their depot."

"Nothing personal." The leader cracked his knuckles. "But Union pays better than curiosity."

Regal was already moving. Fever and blood loss made him slow, but he had mass and he had anger and he had the particular recklessness of a man who'd been fighting losing battles for weeks and had stopped caring about the margins.

His fist connected with the first man's jaw. Solid. The man staggered. Regal grabbed a crate and threw it into the second man's chest, sending him backward into a stack of supplies that collapsed around him.

The leader caught Regal from behind. Arm around his throat. Regal drove his head backward into the man's face, felt the crunch, felt the grip loosen. But the first man had recovered and his fist found Regal's side. The wound. Always the wound.

He went down.

After that: boots. The particular rhythm of men kicking someone who was already on the ground. Professional. Efficient. They knew where to hit to cause maximum pain without killing. This wasn't their first time.

Through the blood and the swelling, Regal could see the woman still sitting at the table. Watching. Drink in hand. The clinical interest of someone observing a process.

"Enough."

One word. Quiet. The room temperature dropped.

The leader turned. Confident. Three against one woman with a drink.

He found himself looking at a pistol that hadn't been in her hand a second ago. Her stance was perfect. The grip steady. The barrel aimed at the center of his chest with the casual precision of someone who'd done this math before and always got the same answer.

"This one's mine now," she said. "Walk away."

"Lady, there's three of us and one of..."

The gunshot was the loudest sound Regal had ever heard in an enclosed space. The leader's shoulder came apart. He spun and hit the concrete screaming.

In the ringing silence that followed, something registered in the back of Regal's battered mind: she'd just spent a round. In a world where ammunition was controlled, tracked, and expensive, she'd just burned one to make a point she could have made with words. That was either reckless or rich. And nothing about this woman read as reckless.

"Two of you," she said. The weapon hadn't moved. "Care to adjust your math?"

They grabbed their screaming companion and ran.

The echo of the gunshot faded. The warehouse settled. The smell of cordite mixed with concrete dust and the copper tang of blood, most of it Regal's.

"Why?" he managed.

"Because I think you and I might have more in common than you realize."

The edges of his vision were going dark. Her voice reached him from a distance that was growing.

"Rest now. When you wake up, we'll discuss how you managed to get this far in life without dying, who you're really hunting, and why I should help you."

He tried to answer. The dark got there first.

✿

He came back slowly. Antiseptic. Clean bandages. A different building. Better lighting. The kind of cleanliness that took resources and planning to maintain.

His wounds had been dressed by someone who knew what they were doing. The fever had broken. For the first time in weeks, his body felt like something that belonged to him instead of something he was fighting against.

Voices through a partially open door. Two women.

"He looks like he tried to solve problems with his face." The voice was flat. Hard-edged. But not emotionless. Something lived in it, under the surface, that was more like scar tissue than absence. The voice of someone who'd learned to strip everything unnecessary from her speech and keep only what cut.

"He freed someone from the Ossuary." The other voice. The cultured accent from the warehouse. "That takes capability."

"Capability." A beat. "Sure. You need anything else, or can I go back to pretending this matters?"

Footsteps. A door closing.

When the woman entered the room an hour later, Regal was sitting up, testing what moved and what didn't. She carried a tray. Food. And coffee. Real coffee, by the smell. The kind that cost more than a week's wages in a border town.

"How do you feel?" she asked.

"Like I was beaten by professionals."

"You were." She poured two cups. "Thank you isn't necessary. But we need to discuss terms."

She handed him the coffee. Her hand was close to his. The heat of the cup transferring through the ceramic and the heat of her proximity registering somewhere in his body that had nothing to do with coffee. He hadn't been handed something warm by another person's hands since

Marta's kitchen. The simple, specific shock of it made him grip the cup harder than he needed to.

"You want to understand what you found," she said. "You want answers about what's happening to whoever you rescued. I can provide both."

"What's the price?"

"Your trust. Your patience. Your willingness to learn that everything you think you know is wrong." She watched him. "The question is whether you can afford that."

No money. No allies. No other leads. The vial still a mystery. The girl's condition getting worse.

"What exactly are you offering?"

"Education. Training. Resources." She leaned back. "But understand this: I'm not interested in your revenge. Going after your enemies directly will get you killed before you accomplish anything. I'm interested in your potential."

"Revenge?" Something cold settled in Regal's chest. "You don't know anything about what I'm after."

"Don't I? Young man breaks into the most secure facility in the territories. Rescues someone important enough to risk everything for. Walks away with classified materials." She studied him. "That's not curiosity. That's personal."

"Personal doesn't begin to cover it."

"Then tell me. Who exactly are you planning to kill?"

The rage was always there. Underneath everything. The same fury that had carried him through the Ossuary's corridors, that had driven him across frozen wastelands, that burned every time he thought about what had been taken from him.

"Shori Ashford."

The name hit the room like a thrown object.

The woman went still. Her coffee cup stopped halfway to her lips. For one beat, something moved behind her eyes that wasn't calculation or assessment. Something older. Something that hurt.

Then it was gone. Replaced by a sharpness that made the air between them feel thin.

"I know of Ashford," she said. Setting the cup down with care. "That's ambitious. She is very dangerous."

"She destroyed my family." Harder than he meant. "My father. My brother. She gave the orders. She sent them to take the girl. Everything traces back to her."

Something flickered across the woman's face. Pain, maybe. Or the shadow of loyalties the room wasn't big enough to hold.

"And if you refuse?" he asked.

"Then you're free to leave. Find your own way, make your own mistakes, die in some ditch before the year's out." She shrugged. "Your choice."

Regal looked into his coffee. The options were darkness in every direction. But one direction had someone standing in it who was warm and capable and offering to keep him alive long enough to matter.

"When do we start?"

She smiled. The first real expression he'd seen from her. Something in it that was not safe and not kind and not anything he had a name for.

"We already have."

She stood. Extended her hand. Not the way someone shakes on a deal. The way someone offers a piece of themselves. First gift. First thread.

"Nessa Kaine."

Her hand was warm. His was not. The contact lasted two seconds, maybe three, and in those seconds Regal's body registered something his brain would spend the next several months failing to process: the specific, overwhelming sensation of being touched by someone who was choosing to touch him. Not pulling him from wreckage. Not checking his wounds. Choosing. Her fingers steady. Her grip measured.

He let go a beat too late. She noticed. Didn't say anything. But the corner of her mouth shifted, just slightly, and something in her green eyes filed the reaction away.

"Regal," he said. "Regal Eldain."

"I know."

Of course she did.

Outside, Braelocke Hollow ground on. Grimy. Tireless. Half-starved for hope.

Inside, Regal made the kind of decision you don't come back from.

PART FOUR

LESSONS IN LEVERAGE

Spring, 2178
Braelocke Hollow to Millhaven Territory

Three weeks into his recovery, the safe house walls were closing in.

Nessa had given him books. Technical manuals about metallurgy. Historical accounts of the Ro'Daerim Event. Theoretical papers on energy extraction that made his head swim with terminology he couldn't hold. He read them because she told him to. Understood maybe a third of what he read. The rest sat in his brain like rocks in a river, water moving around them without wearing them down.

"Theory is the foundation," Nessa said when he complained. "Without understanding the principles, you're just a man with a dangerous toy."

"I don't need theory." Regal paced the small room. Back and forth. A caged animal. "I need to be able to use what I found."

"Do you? Tell me, what's the plan once you understand Thermecine? March up to Shori Ashford's front door and challenge her to single combat?"

The sarcasm stung because it wasn't far from what he'd actually pictured. "I'll find a way."

"You'll find a grave." No hesitation. "Ashford hasn't survived this long by being vulnerable to direct assault. She has resources, connections, security you can't imagine."

The way she said the name. Not the way you say a stranger's name. The way you say a name you've been saying for years, the consonants worn smooth from use. Regal caught it.

"You talk about her like you know her."

A pause. Brief. "I know her reputation. Her methods." Nessa's tone stayed level but something in her shoulders adjusted. "Information networks provide detailed assessments."

"And those networks say she's untouchable?"

"They say she's survived every attempt on her life for nearly a decade." Her eyes held his. "What do your networks tell you?"

The deflection was clean. Redirecting from what she knew back to what he didn't. Regal filed it away.

"Then what's the point of all this?" He gestured at the books. The equipment. The safe house that was starting to feel like a cage with a teacher in it.

"Making you dangerous enough to matter. Smart enough to survive." She stood. Moved to the window. When she turned back, her hand touched his arm. Not a brush. A placement. Fingers settling on the muscle above his elbow with a pressure that was light and specific and lasted exactly long enough to register before she pulled away. "There are easier targets. Union facilities that support her operations. Supply lines. Officials who enable her work."

The place where her hand had been stayed warm after she moved it. Regal's train of thought derailed. He had to rebuild it.

"You want me to go after other people instead."

"I want you to be strategic. Every operation Ashford runs depends on infrastructure. Disrupt that, and you weaken her more effectively than any direct attack."

It sounded right. It felt wrong. Like being shown a detour when you can see the destination.

"Start with the theory," she said. "Then we move to application. But I won't train someone who rushes in without thinking."

⚙

A week later, she took him to the basement.

A workshop hidden beneath the safe house. Precision instruments. Chemical apparatus. Safety equipment. The kind of space that took years of investment to build. Whoever Nessa Kaine was, she'd been doing this for a long time.

"Thermecine," she said, producing a vial similar to what he'd found but clearer. More refined. "Catalytic medium. It doesn't contain energy. It extracts energy from compatible materials and amplifies it through focused intention."

"Compatible materials meaning the steel."

"Among other things. Steel is the most stable. The most controllable." She opened a case of small fragments, each no larger than a coin. "Low-grade samples. Sufficient for learning."

Her demonstration was precise. A drop of Thermecine on the smallest fragment produced a controlled glow. She concentrated, and the glow responded, intensifying, shifting, becoming directed. She shaped the energy with instruments into focused beams, localized heating effects that could cut through metal. Everything controlled. Measured. No wasted output.

"Your turn."

Regal's first attempt flared and died. The fragment sat inert despite everything he threw at it. His frustration built with each failure, and his applications got heavier, cruder, trying to force results through will.

"Concentration," Nessa said. She moved behind him.

Her hands covered his on the focusing rod. Guiding. Her body close enough behind him that he could feel the warmth of her through his shirt. Not pressing against him. Worse. Almost pressing against him. The gap between her body and his small enough that he could feel it like a current, the air between them charged with a proximity that wasn't contact and was somehow more distracting than contact would have been.

"The energy responds to neural patterns. Focused intention." Her voice was near his ear. Not quite at his ear. Close enough that he could feel the warmth of her breath against the side of his neck. "You're thinking like a blacksmith forcing hot iron. Think like a musician tuning an instrument."

"I'm not a musician," he managed. His voice came out wrong. Rougher than he wanted.

"Then learn to be one. Or accept that you'll never progress beyond parlor tricks."

Hours. Attempt after attempt. Her hands correcting his. Her proximity scrambling his focus. Every time he started to find the rhythm, she'd adjust his grip and her fingers would overlap his and his concentration would scatter and he'd have to start over.

He finally held a steady beam for thirty seconds. The fragment glowing with contained energy that felt like his own will made visible. But even in success, it was crude. Raw force channeled through stubbornness rather than precision.

"Better," she said. Her approval hit him in a place that had nothing to do with Thermecine. "Much better. Though you're still using a sledgehammer where a scalpel would serve."

She was still close. Still behind him. He could smell her now. Not perfume. Underneath perfume. The particular warmth of another person's skin, and his body responding to it with a desperation that embarrassed him and wouldn't stop.

He stood up. Put distance between them. Pretended it was about stretching.

She watched him do it. Something in her expression that said she'd noticed. That she'd expected it. That she was counting.

✿

The weeks that followed had a pattern. He could see the pattern. He could not stop the pattern.

Nessa steered his strategic thinking the same way she steered his training: with patient, deliberate redirection. When he asked about Union facilities connected to the Ossuary, she pointed him toward supply depots and administrative centers. When he mentioned Shori Ashford's movements, she suggested focusing on subordinates.

"There's a regional coordinator in Millhaven," she said one evening, laying out a file. "Marcus Veil. Oversees supply logistics for three Ossuary-affiliated facilities. Remove him, and their operations face significant disruption."

Regal studied the file. Veil was a bureaucrat. Soft target. Protected by nothing more than a few guards and his own obscurity.

"This isn't the person who hurt her," he said.

"No. But he enables those who did." She leaned over the table to indicate a map position. Close. Always close. The proximity a constant variable in every conversation, the warmth of her present in every tactical discussion, and Regal's ability to think clearly inversely proportional to the distance between them. "Unless you prefer dramatic gestures over effective action."

He could hear how reasonable it sounded. He could feel how wrong it felt. But the wrongness was buried under the weight of her logic and the heat of her proximity, and every time he almost reached the thought that would have shown him the pattern, she'd shift her position or touch his arm or say his name in a way that sent the thought tumbling away.

✧

Their relationship shifted the way Nessa had designed it to shift.

Late nights reviewing intelligence became conversations that ran past midnight. Regal found himself talking about things he hadn't told anyone. His father's forge. The sound the metal made when the quench was right. The girl's eyes before the Ossuary changed them. The weight of carrying someone through a frozen waste when your own body was failing.

Nessa listened. Asked questions that drew more out of him. Offered small pieces of herself in return, carefully chosen, calibrated to create the illusion of reciprocal vulnerability.

During training, she stood closer. Her hand lingered longer when she corrected his grip. Her praise carried warmth that went past professional satisfaction.

The tension built the way pressure builds behind a dam. Regal could feel it. Every session. Every evening conversation. Every time she was in the room and the air changed and his body responded before his brain had a chance to intervene. Twenty years old and his blood running so hot he couldn't think straight when she looked at him from across a table.

The first kiss was his fault. A training breakthrough. Stable energy extraction, maintained for a full minute. The elation of it, the adrenaline, and Nessa's face inches from his as she said "Excellent," and he kissed her because the distance between them was a problem his body decided to solve without consulting his brain.

She kissed him back. Hard enough that he forgot his own name for three seconds.

Everything after that was hers.

The next evening. Review of energy flow patterns. She'd changed into lighter clothes after training. Thin shirt. The fabric moving with her when she leaned across the table to point at a diagram, and Regal watching the fabric move and hating himself for watching and watching anyway because his eyes had stopped taking orders.

"Am I distracting you?" She'd caught him looking.

"No," he lied. His voice came out broken.

She moved behind his chair. Her hand on his shoulder. Fingers moving through the fabric of his shirt in small patterns that might have been absent-minded if anything Nessa did was absent-minded.

"Focus," she whispered. Close to his ear. Close enough that the word traveled through his nervous system like a lit fuse. "The energy responds to concentration."

He turned in the chair. Her face was right there. Green eyes holding something that looked like want and might have been strategy and he couldn't tell the difference and had stopped trying.

When she kissed him this time, it was nothing like his clumsy attempt from the night before. This was deliberate. Thorough. The kiss of someone who understood exactly what she was doing to him and was doing it on purpose. She kissed him like she was taking inventory of every response his body made, cataloguing what worked, filing it for future reference.

He didn't stand a chance.

"Upstairs," she said against his mouth.

He followed her. The stairs. The lamp-lit room. Her turning to face him as the door closed. Everything that happened next was heat and skin and the overwhelming physical reality of being touched by someone after months of nothing but cold and pain and isolation. He wasn't smooth. He wasn't experienced. He was a man who'd been carrying fire in his chest for weeks and she'd finally opened the door and the fire went where fire goes.

Later. The lamp still burning. Her body against his, warm and real. His heart slamming. The particular silence of a room where something has just changed irreversibly.

"What are you thinking?" she asked.

"That I've never felt anything like this before."

She looked at him. Something in her expression he couldn't read. "Neither have I," she said.

He believed her completely.

From that night, the boundaries dissolved. Training sessions charged with what had happened and what would happen again. Strategic discussions in bed, her skin against his making it impossible to focus on maps and intelligence files. The lines between teacher and student and lover blurred until Regal couldn't find them.

He didn't see the mechanism. Didn't understand that every time he was about to push for Ashford, about to insist on direct action, about to follow the thread that would have led him to the truth, there would be a touch. A look. A night that wiped the thought clean and left him starting over the next morning, one step further from his goal and one step deeper into her.

✧

A month into the affair, Snips appeared at the safe house.

She came from the industrial district like weather: you didn't see her arrive, you just noticed the temperature change. She carried a message pouch that said serious networks.

"Report," Nessa said.

"Three Union patrols asking about Thermecine theft." Snips' voice was flat and hard, the words carrying no extra weight. Economy of speech learned from years of having nothing to waste. "Someone's connecting the depot raid to recent acquisitions. Bounties for information."

Regal looked at her directly. The damaged left eye. The clouded tissue that caught light wrong. The scar topography around it that told a story of specific, deliberate violence. The one good eye, hazel-green, moving through the room with the mechanical precision of someone who'd learned to see the whole world through half the usual equipment.

He didn't look away. Didn't flinch. Just met her gaze the way he'd meet anyone's gaze: steady, direct, because looking away from damage was just another kind of cowardice and he'd had enough cowardice for one lifetime.

Snips registered it. Something shifted behind the good eye. Not warmth. Recalculation. The brief, silent reassessment of someone who'd been read one way by everyone for years and was suddenly being read differently. Her hand went to her wrist. Rubbed at something that wasn't there.

"How much?" Nessa asked.

"Enough to make people interested. Not enough to make them stupid." Snips' attention moved off Regal and back to the briefing. "Your boytoy's face is on wanted notices in four settlements."

Regal flinched.

"Which settlements?"

The locations Snips listed were all along routes toward the capital. Toward Shori Ashford. The message was clear: his original target had just gotten harder to reach.

"Recommendations?" Nessa asked.

"Lay low. Change appearance. Or give them someone else to chase." The good eye flicked to Regal once more. Clinical. "Could always arrange for him to have an accident. Clean up the loose ends with surgical precision."

The way she said it suggested professional specialty, not figure of speech.

"Not yet," Nessa said. Regal felt the chill of how casually she considered the option. "He's proving useful."

"I'm sure he fits right in," Snips said.

"In every way," Nessa replied.

The air in the room changed. Regal's jaw tightened.

After Snips left, he turned on Nessa. "You just told her we're sleeping together."

"Snips is a friend." Nessa closed the distance between them. Stood close enough that his anger had to compete with his body's response to her proximity. "We go back quite a ways."

"Your friend has a difficult past," Regal said. The damaged eye. The trauma visible in every controlled movement. He was trying to stay on the topic. Trying to stay angry. The anger kept slipping because she was close and warm and his blood was twenty years old and didn't care about tactics.

"Snips has proven reliable despite her conditioning." Nessa's tone went carefully neutral. "Sometimes the most broken tools are the most useful ones."

The cruelty of the statement hit him, but before he could follow the thread, she was already redirecting his attention to the intelligence Snips had delivered. The increased Union interest. The need for lower-profile operations. The logic of misdirection.

More distance from his actual goal. More redirection. More delay.

But Regal, saturated in her attention and convinced of her expertise, accepted each turn as tactical wisdom.

The mechanism was invisible because it felt like love.

✿

Spring deepened. The training intensified.

Regal's skill with Thermecine improved, but his applications stayed crude. Where Nessa cut clean lines through metal, he tore jagged holes. Where she generated controlled, sustained energy, he produced raw bursts that got the job done and wasted half the power. Brute efficiency. It worked. It wasn't pretty. She kept telling him to think like a musician and he kept thinking like a man with a hammer, and the results reflected both approaches.

"The Union facility in Greymont," she said one evening. Plans spread across the table. "Regional processing center for genetic materials. Blood samples, tissue records, family lineage data. Everything they need to identify targets with useful traits."

She traced security layouts with her finger. "Destroying their database would blind them across three territories. The files might even contain records connecting specific personnel to specific extractions."

That last part. The connection to who ordered what. The thread that might lead to Ashford.

"When do we move?" Regal asked.

"We don't. You do." She looked up from the plans. "This is your first solo operation. Proof that you've learned enough to matter."

"What about backup?"

"Intelligence updates. Emergency extraction. Communication channels. But the operation is yours." A pause. "Unless you don't think you're ready."

She knew exactly what that challenge would do to his pride. He gave her exactly the answer she'd designed the challenge to produce.

"I'm ready."

"Good. Because this is where we find out if you're actually dangerous, or just another angry young man with expensive toys."

He studied the plans. Memorized every detail. Prepared the way she'd taught him to prepare.

He did not realize he was being sent to destroy evidence that might have led him to Shori Ashford. He thought he was striking a blow.

The spring wind carried new growth through Braelocke's streets. Regal packed his equipment and headed east toward Greymont. Toward a target that served someone else's purpose.

One step. Then another.

PART FIVE

Caelum's Warning

Late Spring, 2178

Greymont Territory to Braelocke Hollow

The Greymont facility burned behind him.

Regal watched it from the ridge, smoke rising into a sky that was already promising rain. The charges had worked exactly as designed. Thermecine-fueled heat cutting through the storage systems with the focused efficiency Nessa had drilled into him for weeks. The automated film archives reduced to slag. The genetic database gone.

For the first time since the Ossuary, he felt like he was making real progress.

But something nagged at him during the walk to the safe house. A splinter in the satisfaction.

The facility had been too easy.

Not the entry. That had been hard enough, maintenance tunnels that tested every ounce of his training. Not the placement, which had required the steady hands and precise timing Nessa had beaten into him. The facility itself. The security. The staffing. A regional processing center for genetic materials across three territories, and it had been protected by a skeleton crew running on what looked like half funding.

Nessa had described it as a critical node. The security said otherwise.

He filed it. Didn't know what it meant yet. But it sat wrong.

The safe house on Greymont's outskirts was a mirror of the one in Braelocke. Sparse. Functional. Regal cleaned his equipment methodically. Catalogued what worked. Packed.

He was securing the last of his gear when a voice came from behind him.

"Impressive work."

Regal's hand went to his knife. He turned.

The man stood just inside the doorway. Not standing, exactly. Leaning. Using the frame the way a man uses a crutch when his body doesn't hold its own weight reliably. He was thin. Wrong-shaped. Not in a way that suggested birth defect or old injury, but in the specific way of someone whose skeleton had been taken apart and reassembled by people who understood the chemistry better than the architecture. His joints sat at angles that were close to normal but not normal, the way a door hangs when the hinges have been removed and rehung slightly off-true.

His eyes were the thing Regal recognized.

Rust. Darker than the girl's. Closer to dried blood than old iron. But the same metallic quality underneath, the same light-catching depth that marked the people who carried that particular inheritance. Except in this man, the quality was wrong. Damaged. The metallic sheen fractured, uneven, as if the processing that had broken his body had also broken whatever made those eyes catch light the way they were supposed to.

"Clean entry," the man continued. "Precise placement. Minimal collateral. Someone taught you well."

"Who are you?" Regal's grip on the knife was tight. But something stopped him from making it a threat. The eyes. The broken body. The particular ruin of someone who'd been through the same machine that had taken the girl.

"My name is Caelum." He moved into the room. The gait was painful to watch. Every step a negotiation between what his joints could do and what they'd been made to do. "You freed me from the Ossuary. Though you probably don't remember. Your mind was elsewhere."

The memory surfaced. A cell. A figure inside, twisted and broken, pointing down the corridor toward where they'd kept her. Regal had cut the restraints and kept moving. Hadn't looked back. Hadn't had time.

"You helped me find her," Regal said.

"I did." Caelum lowered himself into a chair with the careful movements of someone managing a body that punished carelessness. "And I've been watching since. Wanting to see what you'd do with your freedom."

"Following me?"

"Observing. There's a difference." He picked up one of Regal's Thermecine cartridges. Turned it in fingers that bent at angles fingers shouldn't bend. Handled it with surprising precision despite the damage. "The question is whether you understand what you accomplished tonight."

"Genetic database. Processing records. Intelligence that feeds Ossuary operations."

"True. All of it." Caelum set the cartridge down with care. "But incomplete."

The splinter in Regal's satisfaction sharpened. "What do you mean?"

"The facility was understaffed. You noticed."

Regal went still. He hadn't said anything about the staffing.

"Skeleton crew. Half funding. A regional processing center that should have been one of the most secure installations in the territory, and you walked through it." Caelum's broken eyes found his. "That didn't bother you?"

It had bothered him. He'd filed it and moved on. "I assumed deteriorating resources. Budget cuts."

"There are no budget cuts for genetic intelligence. Not in this program." Caelum paused. "That facility was scheduled for closure next month. The equipment was being relocated. The databases you destroyed were being copied to more secure locations."

The words landed.

"You were sent to burn a building that was already being emptied," Caelum said. "And the records you destroyed, the family lineage data, the blood tracing, the chain of custody documents that showed who ordered specific extractions..." He let the silence fill the gap. "That evidence might have led you to the people you actually want to find."

"Nessa said the database was intelligence for future operations."

"It was both. Past and future. Your teacher failed to mention that destroying their records also destroys your ability to prove what they did."

Regal's hands had started shaking. Not from cold. Not from blood loss. From the feeling of ground shifting under his feet.

"She wouldn't do that."

"Wouldn't she?" Caelum tilted his head. The movement was wrong, the neck compensating for joints that didn't rotate properly. "Think about the targets she's given you. Not what she said they were worth. What they were actually worth."

Regal thought. The depot in Braelocke. Davyl's test, not Nessa's. But the targets after: the supply routes. The administrative centers. The bureaucrats.

"Marcus Veil," Caelum said. "The coordinator she was aiming you at next. His replacement was already selected. Trained. Ready to step in without interruption. Killing him would have changed nothing."

"The Millhaven supply depot," Regal said slowly. The ground shifting further. "Secondary logistics hub. She said destroying it would cripple operations."

"Destroying it would have forced them to reroute through primary channels. Faster. More efficient." Caelum watched him arrive at it. "You would have improved their system while believing you were damaging it."

The splinter was a crack now. A crack was becoming a fault line.

"How do you know all this?" Regal's voice had gone flat. Dangerous. The voice he used when he was about to hit something.

"I lived inside that system for years. Listening. Watching how decisions flowed." Caelum's expression carried something that wasn't pity, was closer to recognition. One man who'd been inside the machine speaking to another who was just discovering the shape of it from outside. "I know how it works because it worked on me."

○

Regal stood. The chair scraped back. He needed to move. The room was too small and the information was too big and his body wanted to break something but the only thing in range was a man whose body was already broken.

He paced. The safe house walls close on every side.

"There's something else," Caelum said. "About Ms. Kaine."

"What about her."

"She and Ashford. They were together. Not colleagues. Together. For over a decade." Caelum's voice was careful. Not cruel. The careful delivery of someone handing over something that would do damage no matter how gently it was placed. "The relationship ended roughly three years ago. Not because Kaine stopped caring."

The operational betrayal had hit first. The targets. The misdirection. The strategic futility of everything he'd accomplished.

This hit different.

Slower.

The woman who'd taught him to fight Ashford had been sharing a bed with Ashford for eleven years. The woman who'd kissed him and held him and whispered his name had spent a decade doing the same with the person who'd destroyed his family.

Every touch. Every night. Every time she'd steered him away from a target that would have actually mattered, she'd been protecting the woman she still loved. And she'd kept him blind to it by giving him something that felt like love in return.

He stopped pacing. His hands were at his sides. Fists. The knuckles he'd split on the tavern brawlers starting to ache.

"You're saying she used me."

"I'm saying she has conflicting loyalties. She sees potential in you, but she can't allow that potential to destroy someone she's spent her adult life caring about." Caelum shifted in the chair, his broken body finding a new arrangement that hurt less than the previous one. "She's not evil. She's caught. And caught people make weapons out of the people they're supposed to be protecting."

The word *weapons* stayed in the air.

"She's building a network," Caelum continued. "Creating assets. Preparing for a larger game. You're one piece on a board she's been setting for years."

"And you're what? Another piece?"

"I was. Before the Ossuary broke me." He looked down at his own hands. The twisted fingers. The joints that bent wrong. "Now I'm something else. Something they didn't plan for."

"What do you want from me?"

"Nothing you aren't already considering." Caelum's rust eyes found his. The metallic quality fractured but present. Two men who'd been through the same machine, sitting in a room that smelled like Thermecine residue and the beginning of rain. "You can continue with her. Learn her techniques. Accept her targets. Let her protect Ashford through you."

"Or?"

"Or trust your own judgment. Pursue your real objectives. Accept the risks."

"You're asking me to trust you instead."

"I'm asking you to trust yourself." Caelum stood. The process was slow and painful and he didn't try to hide it. "If you choose to stay with her, I understand. She's... persuasive."

He moved toward the door. The gait that made you look away and then made you look back, because there was something in it that refused to be ashamed of its own damage.

"The path that leads to Ashford directly," Regal said. "What does that look like?"

Caelum stopped at the threshold. "Dangerous. Lonely. No network. No backup. No one to patch you up when the next fight goes wrong." He looked back. "But every target would be yours."

He left. The darkness outside took him back the way it had given him up.

✻

Regal sat in the safe house until dawn.

The equipment Nessa had provided laid out in front of him. The Thermecine cartridges. The focusing tools. The techniques she'd drilled into his hands over weeks of close-quarters training, her body behind his, her voice in his ear, her warmth making everything she said sound like truth.

He could verify what Caelum had told him. Check the facility schedules. Investigate the targets. Confirm or deny the Nessa-Ashford relationship through independent sources.

Verification meant admitting the possibility. And the possibility was a door he'd been standing in front of for weeks without opening. The targets that felt too easy. The deflections when he mentioned Ashford. The way every time he got close to pushing for direct action, there was a touch, a look, a night that reset him.

He'd been seeing it. He hadn't been letting himself see it.

Dawn came through the window. Gray. The rain that Greymont's sky had been promising was arriving.

He made his choice.

He gathered his equipment. Packed. Started the route back to Braelocke Hollow. Back to Nessa. Back to the training and the targets and the woman who'd built herself into the architecture of his days until removing her would mean tearing the whole structure down.

Not because he trusted her. That was done.

Because he wasn't ready. Not for Ashford. Not for Caelum's dangerous, lonely path. Not for operating alone in a world that had proven, repeatedly and specifically, that it would kill him if he gave it the chance.

The techniques were real. The power was genuine. Only the direction had been compromised. He'd take the education. Watch for the manipulation. Keep his own counsel about where the road actually ended.

And when he was strong enough, when the gap between his ability and his target had closed enough to make the attempt something other than suicide, he'd make his own choices.

The walk back took three days. Spring pushing through the frozen ground. Regal moving through the countryside using the techniques Nessa had taught him, her methods keeping him alive while he carried the knowledge that her methods were also keeping him caged.

The safe house appeared on the third evening. Smoke from the chimney. Lights in the windows. Nessa inside, waiting with debriefing questions and mission analysis and the next target and the particular closeness that would make him forget, for another few hours, that he was being used.

Regal approached with the pace of a man who'd learned to look the same when everything underneath had changed.

He opened the door.

Part Six

THE FIRST WIN

Early Summer, 2178
Braelocke Hollow to Redbrook Valley

Everything looked different now.

Same safe house. Same equipment. Same maps pinned to the walls, same Thermecine cartridges lined up on the workbench. Same woman reviewing his Greymont report with professional satisfaction, praising his precision, his clean escape.

Same warm approval that made his chest tighten despite everything Caelum had told him.

"The Greymont database contained genetic profiles from three territories," Nessa said. "Eliminating that intelligence will protect thousands of potential targets."

"How do you know what it contained?"

The question came out before he could stop it. She glanced up. Something flickered behind her eyes. Brief. The micro-adjustment of someone choosing words.

"Intelligence networks. Same sources that identified it as a target." She set down the report. "Why?"

"Just curious about verification."

"Verification comes from multiple sources. Cross-referenced. Analyzed." Her tone stayed casual, but the emphasis landed on *reliable enough* in a way that could cover anything from solid confirmation to educated guesswork. "It's not perfect, but it's reliable enough for planning."

He let it go. Direct confrontation would reveal his hand. Instead he watched. The way she paused before answering. The careful phrasing. The slight tension in her shoulders when his questions got too specific.

He catalogued. He waited.

Weeks passed. Training escalated. Nessa pushed harder, introduced applications that took his crude force and tried to shape it into something more precise. He learned. Improved. His Thermecine work was still blunt, still wasteful, but the results were getting bigger.

He also tested. Small probes disguised as curiosity. Questions about her sources. Requests for details about target verification. Each time, the same deflection. Smooth. Professional. Redirecting from what she knew back to what he should be doing.

He noticed them all now. Filed them alongside Caelum's warnings in a growing dossier of evidence he wasn't ready to use.

"There's a Union convoy moving through the Redbrook Valley next week," Nessa said one evening. Route maps spread on the table. "High-value transport. Scientists and researchers moving between secure facilities."

"What kind of scientists?"

"The kind who design programs like the ones that took the girl you saved." Her finger traced the convoy's path. "Eliminating them would set back their biotechnology development by months."

The mission felt different from the others. Not bureaucrats. Not supply depots. Scientists who actually built the systems that caused the suffering. For the first time, Nessa was pointing him at something that mattered.

Or seemed to.

He took the mission anyway. Because even if it was another misdirection, the convoy might contain intelligence he could use. And because saying no would tell Nessa he'd stopped trusting her aim.

❖

Two days scouting the Redbrook Valley. Timing guard rotations. Mapping sight lines. The narrow valley where the road curved between steep hillsides gave him cover, elevation, and a kill zone that would neutralize the escort vehicles before they could organize a response.

He positioned his equipment the way Nessa had taught him. Thermecine charges calibrated to disable, not destroy. Focused pulses aimed at electrical systems and wheel assemblies. The precision work that she valued.

Dawn. The convoy appeared on the valley road. Three vehicles. Lead escort. Main transport. Rear guard.

Regal hit the lead vehicle first. Thermecine pulse straight into the engine block. The electrical system fried. Sparks sprayed from under the hood and the vehicle died on the road, momentum carrying it sideways into the drainage ditch.

The main transport next. Charges under the road surface, preset. The wheels didn't melt so much as seize. The steel rims fusing to the axle housings in a burst of focused heat that dropped the vehicle onto its belly. The sound of metal screaming against asphalt.

The rear guard managed one radio transmission. One. His Thermecine burst hit their communications array and the equipment came apart in a shower of sparks and melted solder.

Three vehicles. Neutralized. No fatalities.

It worked. It wasn't pretty.

Regal moved through the disabled convoy with his knife out and his senses running at full burn. The scientists were exactly what Nessa had described. Researchers. Lab coats under their travel clothes. Files and equipment and the particular institutional arrogance of people who'd never expected to be touched by the consequences of their work.

He secured intelligence materials. Photographed documents. Recorded serial numbers. Worked fast because the radio transmission meant response teams were coming and the clock had started the moment he'd hit the lead vehicle.

Then he found it.

One file. Thinner than the others. Administrative notes and transfer authorizations. Routine paperwork except for the designation printed across the top in neat clinical lettering.

Subject 437-A.

The memory hit like a fist.

The label. On the tubing. Attached to her arm in the laboratory, the machines drawing from her blood. He'd seen it during the rescue. Had been too focused on cutting her free, too desperate to register anything that wasn't an obstacle or an exit. The designation had passed through his awareness and disappeared.

Now it was in his hands again. On paper. In a file carried by scientists who'd been involved in her case specifically. Not abstract programs. Not institutional systems. Her. The girl with the rust-colored eyes who'd curled into his coat in a frozen shack and whispered "please, too tired."

Reduced to a subject number in their filing system.

Regal's hands shook. Not from cold. Not from exertion. From the specific rage of holding proof that the people who'd catalogued his family like specimens were real, identifiable, reachable.

He took everything. Stuffed the files into his pack. Got out of the valley before the response teams arrived.

For the first time since Braelocke, this felt real.

⚙

Back at the safe house, the captured materials spread across the table like a map to somewhere he'd been trying to reach for months. Personnel names. Facility connections. Protocols that linked specific scientists to specific programs.

And references to someone designated only as "Director A." Oversight authority for genetic research across multiple territories. The documents suggested this person had direct knowledge of the experiments conducted on Subject 437-A. Maybe direct responsibility.

"This is significant," Nessa agreed when he showed her. But her enthusiasm was muted. She skimmed the documents with the practiced speed of someone who was looking for specific things rather than discovering new information. Her eyes moved past the pages containing the girl's designation without lingering.

"Director A has been mentioned in other materials," she said. "Very high-level. Extremely well-protected."

"Can we identify them?"

"Possibly. With additional intelligence. Cross-referencing." She set the files aside. Too quickly. "But someone at that level isn't accessible through direct action. We'd need to work up through subordinates."

The same strategy. Indirect approaches. Peripheral targets. Long campaigns.

But this time Regal had proof that the indirect path could yield real connections. The Subject 437-A file wasn't symbolic. It was specific. And Nessa's muted reaction to it, the way she'd skimmed past the designation without comment, the way she was already redirecting toward subordinates and organizational charts, all of it landed on the foundation Caelum had built.

She didn't want him following this thread.

That night. The lamp burning low. Her body against his. The heat of her familiar and confusing, everything good about it contaminated by everything he now suspected.

"What are you thinking about?" she asked. Her hand on his chest.

"You," he said.

True. Not in the way she thought.

She kissed him. He kissed her back. Because whatever she was hiding, his body hadn't gotten the message yet. His body still responded to her warmth the way it had from the beginning: without consultation, without permission, without caring that the warmth might be calculated.

"Didn't it?" he thought afterward, staring at the ceiling while she slept. "Didn't it have to be real?"

He didn't have an answer.

✧

Three days later, Snips walked in.

No warning. No knock. She appeared in the safe house the way weather appears: you didn't see it coming, you just noticed the air had changed.

"Union security sweep." Hard voice. Clipped. "Multiple facilities. Coordinated timing. They're purging records, reassigning personnel, new security protocols across the board."

"Response to the convoy?" Regal asked.

"Response to information leakage." Snips' one good eye found Nessa and stayed there. "Someone told them exactly what was taken. Who had access. How it might be used."

The room went cold.

"Who had access to our intelligence?" Regal asked quietly.

"Just us." Nessa's voice was steady. Her hands were not. The tremor was small but present, a crack in the composure that said more than any confession. "Unless the materials contained tracking elements we didn't detect."

"Or unless someone reported the capture to Union contacts." Snips hadn't blinked. The good eye locked on Nessa with the flat precision of someone who understood exactly how betrayals like this worked. Because she'd been built by one. "Someone who wanted the investigation stopped before it reached certain people."

Regal felt the heat rise. Temple throbbing. His body tensing toward violence the way it always tensed toward violence when the alternative was feeling something he couldn't hit. He flinched forward. Caught himself. Felt Nessa's hand on his shoulder.

He shook it off.

Crossed the room. Stood with his back to both of them.

Another dead end. Another promising lead dissolved the moment it became useful. The Subject 437-A file, the first genuine connection to the people who'd taken his family, neutralized within days of being captured.

"The evidence is compromised," Nessa said. "Whatever we learned, we have to assume they know we learned it. Any operation based on this intelligence is now extremely dangerous."

"Or impossible," Snips said. "If they know what you know, they can predict what you'll do. Set traps." A pause. The good eye shifting to Regal. "Dispose of playthings."

Regal's fists tightened at his sides. Snips saw it. The smirk that touched the corner of her mouth was small and cold and said: *I'm right and you know it.*

He shook Nessa's hand off his shoulder again. She hadn't tried to put it back. She'd just moved closer.

✿

Regal lay awake that night. Nessa asleep beside him. Her breathing slow and even.

Three operations. Each one appearing successful. Each one advancing his objectives not at all. And now the first time he'd captured real intelligence, it was immediately exposed and erased.

The pattern wasn't subtle anymore. It was a wall he kept walking into because the woman lying next to him kept turning him toward it.

He thought about getting up. Packing. Walking out the door and into Caelum's dangerous, lonely, honest path.

He stayed in bed.

Not because he trusted her. Not because the pattern wasn't clear. Because the heat of her body against his was the only warmth he had, and walking into the cold alone was a decision his muscles remembered making once before, carrying someone through frozen wastelands, and the memory of that cold was still in his bones.

The mechanism was still working. Even now. Even knowing.

He closed his eyes. Didn't sleep.

PART SEVEN

THE WILDCARD

Summer, 2178
Millhaven Territory

— ❖ —

The argument happened on a Tuesday evening. Like most things that end relationships, it started with a question.

"There's another option," Regal said.

Nessa looked up from the intelligence files she was spreading across the table. More bureaucrats. More administrators. More peripheral targets that would consume months and accomplish nothing.

"Which is?"

"Direct action against the source. Shori Ashford herself."

The name did what it always did. Nessa's body went still for a beat too long. The tell she'd never managed to hide, no matter how many other tells she'd trained out of her reactions.

"We've discussed this."

"Not really. You've told me it's impossible. I've accepted it. That's not the same as discussing it."

"It's suicide, Regal."

"Is it? Or is it just difficult?"

"Both. The distinction doesn't matter if you're dead." She gathered the files. Her hands trembled. Not enough for someone who wasn't watching to notice. He was watching. "I won't train someone to commit elaborate suicide."

"Your concern seems personal." He held her gaze. "Almost like you're protecting her rather than protecting me."

"I'm protecting you from decisions based on emotion rather than strategy."

"Are you? Or are you protecting someone you care about from the consequences of what they've done?"

Silence. The safe house around them holding its breath.

That silence was the loudest thing Nessa had ever said to him.

✧

He contacted Webb that night.

Not through Nessa's channels. Through an emergency protocol she'd taught him, using a contact she'd mentioned once and never followed up on. Dr. Marcus Webb. Senior researcher at the Millhaven Biotechnology Institute. Someone connected to Ossuary programs who might provide actionable intelligence.

The message was simple: *Interested in discussing mutual concerns regarding research programs. Confidential meeting possible.*

Webb's response came within hours. Too fast. *Thursday evening. Millhaven Public Library, archives section. Come alone.*

Regal knew it was probably a trap. Went anyway. Because direct action was the only language he spoke fluently, and he'd been speaking someone else's language for too long.

✧

The Millhaven library was a pre-collapse building that had survived through sheer structural stubbornness. The archives occupied the basement. Stacks deep enough to swallow sound.

Webb was thin, fifties, nervous in a way that looked rehearsed. His eyes kept flicking toward specific positions in the stacks at calculated intervals. The careful timing of someone who was stalling for something.

"What are you hoping to accomplish?" Webb asked.

"Information. About Ossuary programs. Personnel. Specifically about research involving children."

Webb provided exactly what Regal needed. Names. Facilities. Confirmation that Ashford was personally responsible for the programs. That Dr. Efram Odell designed them but Ashford perfected them. That the Ossuary was systematic transformation, not just research.

It was perfect. Too perfect.

"How do you know all this?" Regal asked.

"I was involved in the early stages." Guilt on his face. But the posture was wrong. Practiced. "I've been documenting everything. Preparing for disclosure."

He reached into his jacket. Produced a storage case. "Everything is here. Operational details. Personnel files. Authorization chains."

The realization arrived a beat before the security team.

Too convenient. Too exactly what he needed. Bait shaped like answers.

They came from the stacks. Professional. Private contractors. The kind of equipment that said serious money. They had him restrained before he could draw his knife, pressure points sending paralysis through his arms and legs with the efficiency of people who'd done this many times.

"Dr. Webb. Thank you for your cooperation."

Webb's nervous mask evaporated. Cold professionalism underneath. "Everything proceeded as planned."

The Thermecine vial was removed from Regal's jacket. His weapons. His communications. Stripped clean with surgical efficiency.

He should have been angry. Should have been afraid. Instead, as the paralysis spread and his vision narrowed, a cold clarity settled over him. He'd walked into this trap because direct action was all he knew. And the trap existed because Nessa had predicted exactly that.

She knew him. Better than he knew himself. Better than he'd wanted to believe.

The dark took him.

✧

He woke in a medical facility. Clean. White. Equipment humming. His wounds dressed. His restraints removed, though the marks they'd left were still visible on his wrists.

His effects were on the table beside him. All of them. Weapons. Communications. Even the Thermecine vial. Returned undamaged.

Either they were confident in their security, or they wanted him to have everything he needed to leave.

The note was in her handwriting.

Regal—

Your independence was inevitable. I hoped to delay it.

The intelligence Webb provided is accurate. Ashford is responsible. The facilities are real. The names are correct.

Using it will require capabilities you don't possess. Webb's cooperation was bait, not generosity.

You have a choice. Return to my guidance. Or pursue your vendetta independently.

The door opens in one hour.

For what it's worth—not everything between us was calculated. Some of it was real. More real than I should have allowed.

Choose wisely.

—N

Regal read it twice. The first time for the words. The second time for what was underneath them.

More real than I should have allowed.

He didn't know if that was true. Didn't know if it mattered. What mattered was the cold settling in his chest. Not anger. Past anger. The flat, clear understanding of a man who'd finally seen the mechanism and couldn't unsee it.

She'd taught him to read people. To identify needs. To provide what someone wanted just long enough to serve a purpose. To build connections that could be leveraged. To make someone feel valued while steering their actions.

She'd taught him how to use people.

And she'd done it by using him.

The lesson she hadn't meant to teach was the one that stuck.

✧

The door opened in exactly one hour. Corridor. Exit. No guards. No obstacles. Even his freedom was choreographed.

Outside: Millhaven under an overcast sky. Rain starting. Warm rain that soaked through his shirt and into the places where decisions lived.

He could go back. Return to Braelocke. Accept her guidance on terms that acknowledged the manipulation. Access to training, intelligence, support. The warm bed and the warm body and the warm lie that was easier than the cold truth.

He stood in the rain and felt it on his skin and thought about his father's forge. The way steel changed when you heated it past a certain point.

Not just softer. Different. The molecular structure rearranging into something that couldn't go back to what it was before.

He'd passed that point.

Regal walked.

Not back to Braelocke. Not toward Ashford. Into the territory between. The space where nobody was watching and nobody was steering and every step was his and every target would be his and the cost of that ownership would be carried in a body that had already learned to carry more than it should.

He was rejecting her control. Not her education.

The techniques were real. The power was genuine. The ability to read people, to find their vulnerabilities, to build leverage. All of it stayed. What he was leaving behind was the illusion that any of it had been given to him out of care.

The rain came harder. Regal walked into it.

He carried everything she'd taught him. He trusted none of it. He trusted nothing.

That was the education. The real one. The one she'd been teaching him since the moment she extended her hand in a warehouse and said her name like it was a gift.

One step. Then another.

NESSA CODA

The Shape of Fire

Early Spring, 2179

Private Chambers, Stonewake Group Safehouse
Millhaven Territory

Webb's report was on my desk. I'd stopped reading it hours ago.

The details were predictable. Regal had taken the bait exactly as projected. Revealed the depth of his suspicions exactly as his psychological profile suggested he would. Chosen independence exactly as I'd anticipated when I'd designed the scenario.

I should have been satisfied. The operation had performed within acceptable parameters. The asset had been redirected from targets that mattered toward targets that didn't. His brief period of genuine progress had been identified and neutralized before it could produce actionable results. The system was intact. The objective was achieved.

I composed the operational report with the clinical precision the work demanded.

Subject: Asset Reassignment

R. Eldain has been released from developmental control. Current trajectory suggests independent operations targeting Ossuary programs and associated personnel. Recommend monitoring without intervention.

Assessment: Subject demonstrates capacity for strategic thinking, tactical innovation, and moral clarity that may prove valuable in extended operations. Uncontrollable but potentially effective if properly motivated.

Note: Subject possesses genuine cause for grievance against Field Director Ashford. Personal vendetta may align with institutional objectives if circumstances develop appropriately.

Recommend maintaining passive observation.

—Architect

Professional. Comprehensive. The language of someone managing assets and calculating probabilities.

I signed it and set down my pen and stared at the wall and waited for the satisfaction to arrive.

It didn't.

⚙

The thing I hadn't planned for was this: the quiet.

Not the safe house. The safe house had always been quiet. Sparse rooms. Functional equipment. The particular silence of a space designed for one person to work in without distraction.

The quiet was inside me. The place where his voice used to be. His breathing at night. The weight of him beside me in the narrow bed, the heat of his body against my back when he slept, which he did with one arm across me as if he was afraid I'd leave before morning.

He always held me like that. Like I was something he'd found in the wreckage and couldn't believe his luck.

I sat at my desk and tried to write the next operational assessment and my hands wouldn't move.

This was not in the plan.

The plan was specific. I'd executed versions of it before. Find someone broken. Identify the need. Provide what the need demanded: purpose, training, direction. Add physical intimacy as a bonding mechanism when the emotional architecture was sufficiently load-bearing. Use the intimacy to deepen dependence, redirect focus, maintain control of the asset's operational trajectory.

Standard methodology. I'd used it on others. Not with this exact mechanism, not always with the body, but the structure was the same. Find the need. Fill it. Aim the result.

With Regal, the mechanism was his isolation. Months of cold and pain and carrying weight alone. A young man who hadn't been touched by anyone who wasn't trying to hurt him since he'd carried his sister through the frozen waste. I offered warmth. Proximity. The specific physical comfort of being wanted.

And he'd responded exactly as predicted. Overwhelmed. Confused. Dependent. His body making decisions his mind couldn't override. Every touch I calibrated, every escalation I timed, every night I spent with him serving the dual purpose of deepening his attachment and exhausting the energy he might otherwise have directed toward Ashford.

Textbook. Clinical. Effective.

Except.

Except somewhere between the first handshake in the warehouse and the last night in the safe house, the mechanism had turned. Not on him. On me.

I didn't notice it happening. That was the worst part. I was so focused on monitoring his responses, cataloguing his tells, measuring the depth of his attachment against my operational requirements, that I forgot to monitor my own.

The way his hands shook the first time he reached for me. Not from cold. From the overwhelming newness of being touched by someone who was choosing to touch him. I'd registered it as data. Filed it under vulnerability assessment. Used it to calibrate the next escalation.

But I'd also felt it. The trembling. The raw, unguarded need of a person who'd been alone too long. And something in me had responded not as an operator but as a woman who'd been alone too long herself.

His hands on my skin. Rough. Clumsy. Honest in a way that nothing in my life had been honest in years. He touched me like he was afraid he'd break me and afraid he'd lose me and both fears were the same fear and it was the most genuine thing anyone had offered me since Shori had stopped meaning it.

I'd told myself it was strategy. Through every night, every morning, every moment his young body pressed against mine with that fierce, untempered hunger. Strategy. Control. Operational necessity.

I was lying.

And I didn't know I was lying until he walked out of that facility in the rain and something inside my chest collapsed like a structure that had been load-bearing without anyone noticing, and now it was gone and the building was still standing but it wasn't the same building and it would never be the same building again.

He left cold. Carrying my methods. Carrying nothing of me that he wanted to keep.

I sat at my desk in a safe house in Millhaven and felt the specific, devastating grief of a woman who'd set a trap and caught herself in it.

✦

The pattern was clear now. Laid out in front of me like evidence at a trial where I was both prosecutor and defendant.

Snips. Anne Calder. Found her broken. Shaped her trauma into loyalty. Taught her that violence was the only reliable language. Turned a girl who'd helped grandmothers with bags into something that flinched from kindness because I'd taught her that kindness was just another form of manipulation.

When Regal had looked at Snips with simple respect, met her damaged eye without flinching, she'd been so thrown she'd nearly fled the room. Because I'd built her in a world where respect was always a weapon, and she no longer had the wiring to receive it as anything else.

Regal. Found him broken. Shaped his grief into direction. Used his body's need for warmth to keep him dependent on my proximity while I steered him away from everything that mattered to him. Taught him, through my own methods, that people are tools and intimacy is leverage and no one operates from genuine feeling.

Two weapons. Two broken people I'd found and broken further. Both of them carrying my lessons into a world that needed hope, and I'd given them sophistication instead.

I was becoming what Shori had already become. Someone who justified breaking people by pointing at the larger good it served.

But there was a difference between Shori and me. A difference I'd only just discovered.

Shori used love as a tool and remained detached. She'd stroked my hair and called a mutilated girl a pawn and meant both gestures equally. She never lost control of her own mechanism. Never got caught in her own architecture. She was the better architect because she was the colder one.

I wasn't cold enough.

I'd tried to use love as a tool and the love had become real and I hadn't noticed until the tool walked out the door and took the warmth with it.

That was the revelation that settled in my chest like ice. Not that I'd failed to control Regal. That I'd failed to control myself.

✦

I wrote to Snips.

Snips—

The boy chose independence. He'll probably be dead within six months, but if he survives longer, he might become genuinely dangerous.

Keep distant tabs. Not for protection. For information. If he manages to accomplish something meaningful, I want to know.

And if he ever comes looking for allies who understand what he's really fighting, point him toward people who remember that some wars are worth the cost.

I'm sorry. For what I did to you. For what I turned you into. For finding you broken and choosing to break you further instead of helping you heal.

You both deserved better from me.

—N

I sent it and sat in the quiet and thought about the two people I'd sent into the world carrying my damage.

A chime on my communication device. Incoming message. The encryption was familiar. Too familiar.

Nessa—

I know about the boy. About your investigation into Ossuary operations. About your growing concerns regarding program expansion.

I'm not writing to threaten you. I'm writing to remind you that some games have consequences that extend beyond the players.

Think carefully about what you're building and who you're building it for.

—S

Shori knew. Of course she knew. Her networks were too comprehensive for my activities to stay hidden forever. The question was whether she considered me a manageable problem or an existential threat.

I read her letter three times. Each time the words did something different to me. The first read was operational assessment. The second was personal grief, because I could hear her voice in the phrasing, the particular cadence of a woman I'd shared a bed with for eleven years.

The third read was the one where I understood that the next time we met, it would be as enemies.

I didn't write back.

There was nothing to say that wouldn't be a weapon or a confession, and I was done handing out both.

☼

I sat in the safe house as the light changed. Winter barely yielding to spring outside the windows. Millhaven carrying on below in its eternal negotiation between survival and commerce.

Inside, I opened the bottom drawer of my desk. The file I'd been building for three years. Intelligence on Shori's operations. The Ossuary programs. The scope of what she was constructing. Evidence I'd gathered and documented and done nothing with because I couldn't accept that the woman I'd loved had become the thing that needed to be stopped.

I'd known for months. Had done nothing.

Regal had forced the choice. Not through his principles or his courage or his moral clarity. Through his departure. Through the specific, personal devastation of watching someone walk away and discovering that you'd given them the means to walk and the reason to walk and the cold to walk in, and you'd done all of it on purpose, and the only part you hadn't done on purpose was the part where it destroyed you.

I closed the drawer. Opened it again. Pulled out the file.

Three years of pretending I was protecting Shori while building the architecture to bring her down. Three years of telling myself the contradiction was strategy when it was just cowardice. The same cowardice that had let me use a twenty-year-old boy's body to keep him in a cage, and then be surprised when the cage felt empty after he left.

The network was already in place. Hull's contacts. The shipping manifest woman. The guards I'd re-employed. The coded frequencies and debts and quiet people who could be trusted to be elsewhere when necessary. Snips. And now, somewhere in the territories, Regal. Uncontrolled. Unpredictable. Dangerous in ways I'd built and ways I hadn't.

All the pieces. Just no one willing to set them in motion.

I picked up my pen. Started with the first message. Then the second. Then the third. Building the architecture of a war that would take years and cost everything and might not accomplish anything except proving that I'd finally chosen a side.

The safe house settled around me. The quiet that used to be his breathing and his weight and his warmth was just quiet now. The particular silence of a room with one person in it who used to have two.

Outside, winter was losing its grip. Inside, I was tightening mine.

On everything except the thing I'd already lost.

ABOUT THE AUTHOR

JT Baldwin spent thirty years carrying the world of Blood & Steel before he ever wrote it down. The first sketches lived in notebooks shared with his twin brother — game designs, comic characters, half-built mythologies that never quite let him go. They matured in silence through a career that took him from military service to long-haul trucking across the country, the kind of work that leaves a person alone with their thoughts for ten hours at a time. The characters traveled with him.

The Blood & Steel saga foundation is built on three interlocking series: the Ironforged novels, beginning with *Wilted Crowns*; *The Palisade Journals*, a five-novella collection charting the decades of conspiracy and resistance that shape everything to come; and *Forged in Blood & Steel*, an ongoing collection of short stories from the world. He believes the best stories leave readers with something worth thinking about long after the last page — and that the second read should be richer than the first.

He lives in southeastern Minnesota with his wife, where the world keeps growing and the winters are too damn cold and long.

www.ingramcontent.com/pod-product-compliance
Lightning Source LLC
Chambersburg PA
CBHW022045170626
46808CB00003B/1375